Word List

Here is a list of words that might make it easier
to read this book. You'll find them in boldface
the first time they appear in the story.

| | |
|---|---|
| tropical | TRO-pi-kuhl |
| fiercest | FEARS-ist |
| Cayman | kay-MAN |
| Buccaneer | buh-kuh-NEAR |
| Defiant | di-FEYE-uhnt |
| cutlasses | KUHT-luh-sis |
| scoundrels | SKOUN-druhls |
| frustration | fruhs-TRAY-shun |
| boulders | BOHL-ders |
| determination | di-ter-muh-NAY-shun |
| serum | SEAR-uhm |
| twentieth | TWEN-tee-ith |
| century | SEN-shuh-ree |

# Barbie™

## High Sea Adventure

BARBIE and associated trademarks are owned by and used under license from Mattel, Inc. © 1999 Mattel, Inc. All Rights Reserved. Published by Grolier Books, a division of Grolier Enterprises, Inc. Story by Rita Balducci. Photo crew: Dennis DiLaura, Patrick Kittel, Lin Carlson, Barb Miller, Dave Bateman, Susan Cracraft, and Lisa Collins. Produced by Bumpy Slide Books. Printed in the United States of America. ISBN: 0-7172-8860-9

GROLIER
BOOKS

## Chapter One

"Midge, duck!" Barbie shouted.

Midge felt something hit her head. "Owww!" she cried. Then everything went black.

"Are you all right?" she heard a voice ask.

Midge touched her head and blinked in the bright sunlight. Her friend Barbie was leaning over her, gently pressing a cool cloth to Midge's forehead. Beside her knelt Midge's father, Dr. Dawson.

"Easy does it, my dear," her father said. "That's quite a bad bump you have."

"I'm so s-s-sorry, miss," a young sailor

stammered. He pointed toward the barrel he had been carrying. "I didn't see you coming."

Midge tried to smile to show the young man she wasn't upset. "Accidents happen," she told him. She took a deep breath. "I'm fine. Really."

Dr. Dawson frowned. "I hope I didn't make a mistake in bringing you with me on this trip," he said. "Everyone told me a navy ship was no place for a young lady."

Midge stood up quickly, forgetting the pain in her head. "Oh, no, Father! It's just a little bump. I feel better already."

Dr. Dawson chuckled. "All right, Midge," he said. "Just be careful."

Barbie and Midge watched him walk back toward his quarters below the ship's deck. As soon as he disappeared from view, Midge sank back to the hard, wooden floor with a moan.

"Midge!" Barbie cried in alarm.

"It's not my head," Midge said. Her face

was a pale shade of green. "I'm seasick!"

"Poor Midge," Barbie said kindly. Her friend had been having a difficult time since they had come aboard the *Seaflower*. Midge had begged her father for weeks to take them on this trip. She had always longed for an exciting adventure at sea. But now Midge couldn't wait to set foot on dry land again!

"Are you sorry I talked you into this?" Midge asked her friend glumly.

"Sorry? Don't be silly," Barbie answered. "It reminds me of the sailing I did when I was a little girl. And this trip is so exciting! We're traveling across the sea to a beautiful **tropical** island! What could be more wonderful?"

Midge groaned. "A floor that doesn't rock, for one thing," she sighed.

Barbie could feel the ship bobbing up and down under her feet. She laughed and helped her friend stand up. "I know someone who can take your mind off your stomach. Come on!"

Midge and Barbie lifted the hems of their heavy woolen skirts as they walked across the *Seaflower*'s deck. The ship's four huge sails flapped in the breeze over their heads. All around them, sailors were hard at work. They let out sails, adjusted ropes, and watched the sky for changes in the weather. The smell of the sea was in the air, and it made Barbie feel full of energy.

Barbie watched a sailor quickly climb one of the ship's masts to a small platform called a crow's nest. "I wish I could do that," she said. "Imagine spotting a pirate ship!"

"Please!" Midge begged, covering her ears. "I feel sick enough already!"

The friends ducked through a dark doorway and carefully made their way down a narrow wooden staircase. The lower deck of the ship was damp and smelly, and it seemed to rock more with the waves. Their hands helped guide them along the dim passage. Soon they came to another doorway that led into the ship's kitchen, or galley. An old sailor was seated at a table, soaking strips of dried beef in salt water.

"Ahoy there!" the cook cried merrily. "To what do I owe this unexpected pleasure?"

"Midge needs cheering up," Barbie told him.

Mick's blue eyes twinkled. "Aye, aye, lassie!" he said. Then he asked, "Do you know this one?" He burst into a merry song.

*Oh, I miss my love*
*when I'm at sea,*
*How I wish that I could hold her!*
*But no one's cuddling up to me*
*But this parrot on my shoulder!*

Mick pretended that a bird on his shoulder was biting his finger. "Aye! The **fiercest** pirate on the seas undone by the likes of a parrot."

Barbie and Midge burst out laughing.

"Mick, only you could make pirates seem funny," Midge declared.

The cook snorted. "Oh, they're a rough lot, all right," he said. "They fly under the skull-and-crossbones flag, the Jolly Roger. They leave their homes, their honor, even their names behind, all for the sake of a bit of treasure."

"Their names?" Barbie asked.

"Sure," Mick replied, adding more beef to the kettle of water. *"Blackbeard. Calico Jack. One-Eyed Pete. Red Beak.* Did you think their *mommies* gave them those names?"

Midge giggled. "I've never heard of Red Beak!" she told him.

"Aye, he's named that because of his big, sunburned nose!" Mick explained.

Midge put her hand on her upset stomach and groaned. "If *I* were a pirate, they'd call me Green Face."

They all laughed.

"Pirates are no laughing matter," said a low voice from the doorway.

The three turned and saw Dr. Dawson standing there. "Don't you remember what Blackbeard did up in Charleston last year? He held the city's most important citizens hostage until he was given medicines for his crew. I came here to tell you that land has been sighted."

Midge and Barbie jumped up. "Are we at the **Cayman** Islands?" they asked together.

The doctor shook his head. "Not yet. We are just passing **Buccaneer** Bay—a well-known pirate hideout. You two stay out of sight until we pass by. Mick will keep you company until it's safe to come above deck."

The worried look on her father's face made it clear to Midge that she should not argue.

As Barbie and Midge watched him go, they tried not to think about the risk they were taking. Several navy ships had recently been robbed by pirates in these same waters. They knew that the *Seaflower* carried lots of valuable goods. But perhaps the most precious of all was the supply of medicines. Dr. Dawson hoped to use them to start a hospital on the island.

"Now, ladies, don't you worry," Mick said. He tried to think of something to take their minds off the danger. He went to a wooden box and brought out a rolled-up map. "Do you know how to read one of these?" he asked.

"Yes," Midge answered. "My father lets me study his maps all the time. It's his own fault I grew up wanting to be a sailor."

"Well, this is a map of the sky," Mick explained to Barbie. "By studying the stars, we know in which direction to sail."

Barbie studied the delicately drawn map. "This is a work of art," she declared.

"Thank you," Mick said proudly. "I've been working on it as a gift for your father," he told

Midge. "I know he collects maps."

Midge and Barbie were impressed. They never would have guessed that the ship's old cook was so skilled. Just then the kettle of beef began to bubble over onto the floor.

Barbie and Midge held their noses.

"Mick, you're a wonderful mapmaker," Barbie said, "and you seem to know everything about pirates, but . . ."

"I'm a lousy cook," Mick laughed. "But I'll make buccaneers of you yet, ladies!"

"Buccaneers!" Midge cried. "I'm no pirate!"

Mick winked. "I'll let you in on a little secret. The word *buccaneer* started out as a fancy name for a person who eats dried beef at sea! So we're all buccaneers."

The three enjoyed another laugh as Mick began to clean up the mess.

## Chapter Two

The next morning, Barbie and Midge were awakened by a shout from above. "Land ho!"

The big wooden ship creaked and shook as fifty sailors raced to the decks. Barbie and Midge quickly dressed and joined the men.

"Oh! How beautiful!" gasped Barbie.

The island's green mountains gently sloped to the sea. The beaches were covered with white sand, and the water sparkled brilliantly in the morning sunlight. A group of dolphins played in the waves, making Barbie and Midge laugh. Suddenly a big splash frightened the playful creatures away. The *Seaflower* had dropped anchor.

The big ship was too heavy to come any closer to the island without getting stuck in the sand. The sailors untied several small rowboats on the deck and carefully lowered them to the water.

"Coming, ladies?" Dr. Dawson asked.

Barbie and Midge gathered their long skirts in their arms. Then they climbed down to the waiting rowboat. It was wet and shaky. But soon they were all seated. A strong sailor rowed them toward the shore, where a small group of people were waving.

Dr. Dawson smiled as they got closer to land. "There's someone here I'd like you both to meet," he told Barbie and Midge.

When the bottom of the rowboat scraped against the soft sand, the sailor jumped out. He held out his arms to Barbie.

"I don't mind getting a little wet," Barbie said, jumping into the shallow water.

Midge allowed the sailor to lift her out of the boat. He waded through the waves, carrying her to dry land.

"Dr. Dawson!" cried a dark-haired young woman in a bright dress. "I am pleased you came back so soon."

The doctor smiled. "Thank you, Miss Rivera," he replied. Then he turned to Barbie and Midge. "I'd like you to meet my daughter, Midge, and her good friend Barbie."

The woman reached out and took their hands. "I am Teresa Rivera," she said.

"Miss Rivera wants to be a nurse," Dr. Dawson explained. "And now she will finally get her chance."

"Please, call me Teresa," she requested. "Would you like to come back to my house to rest from your trip? My family will be so happy to meet you."

Dr. Dawson shook his head. "Thank you,

but there's a lot to do," he said. Then he nodded to Barbie and Midge. "Teresa will see that you stay out of trouble. I'll join you all later."

Teresa smiled as Dr. Dawson walked away. Then she turned to Midge and said, "Your father is a very kind man."

"Yes, he is," Midge agreed.

Teresa led them across the beach to a street paved with cobblestones. The village was bustling with shops, sailors, islanders, and animals. A gentle breeze and shady palm trees kept them cool as they walked.

"It's so crowded for such a small town," Barbie commented.

"There are many ships anchored here," Teresa explained. "A few merchant ships, two navy ships, and some fishing boats. Of course, there's always a pirate ship or two hiding somewhere nearby."

"Pirates!" Barbie and Midge cried together.

Teresa sighed. "They're everywhere these days," she told them. "My family has lost three shiploads of sugarcane to Red Beak. The last ship was returning with the gold paid for a cargo of sugar that had been sold. If another one of our ships is overtaken, we will have nothing. I had hoped the money from the sugar would make it possible for my family to hire help for the farm. Then I would have been free to learn medicine from Dr. Dawson and become a nurse. Without that money, my family needs me to help with the crops." She sighed again.

"Perhaps the navy could find Red Beak's hideout," Barbie offered hopefully. "Then they could recover your family's fortune."

Teresa shook her head. "The navy is already searching for Red Beak. He's captured two navy ships. They have had no luck in finding him or his ship, the **Defiant.** I'm afraid it's hopeless."

Barbie and Midge exchanged looks. They

wished there was some way to help.

The street twisted into a narrow alley. Then Midge pointed. "Look! A mapmaker's shop! Maybe I can get a map for my father."

Barbie and Teresa waited outside while Midge went into the tiny shop. Maps and globes of all kinds were scattered everywhere. The mapmaker's inks had dripped onto the floor in colorful pools, staining the wooden boards. At the moment, the mapmaker was busy with two other customers. Midge couldn't help noticing that they looked like pirates!

While Midge waited for the mapmaker, she examined a large, unfinished map in the back of the shop. Midge leaned forward for a closer look. As she did, she overheard the three men speaking.

"Tell Red Beak the trade is made," the mapmaker whispered. "Go to the mouth of the Little Bear." He glanced back at Midge. She pretended to study a globe, her heart pounding. Would the men realize she had overheard them?

The two customers brushed past Midge as they left the shop, nodding to her. Midge gulped. She was *sure* they were pirates!

Midge bought a map of the Cayman Islands and hurried out. She dragged Barbie and Teresa up the street. Once they were safely out of view of the shop, she told them what she had heard.

"Red Beak again!" Teresa hissed angrily. "He must be hiding nearby. There's going to be trouble soon. I'm sure of it!"

"But what can the message mean?" Barbie asked. "Is there a place called Little Bear nearby?"

"Not that I know of," Teresa admitted. "Although, if I know anything about pirates, it's probably the name of a tavern."

"No," Midge said. "This was a secret. They were whispering. I can't imagine Red Beak would come ashore to a tavern, especially with

the navy on the lookout for him."

"Whatever it means," Barbie replied, "we had better let the captain of the *Seaflower* know. Red Beak and his crew may be planning trouble."

Just then there was a flurry of activity in the street. Dogs barked, and mothers pulled their children close. Two rough-looking men marched up the street. Sharp swords, called **cutlasses,** swung from their belts with each step.

"Those are the men from the shop," Midge said under her breath.

As the men passed, they bowed. "Good day to you, ladies," they said mockingly.

Barbie, Midge, and Teresa stood in place, their chins up and their expressions firm. The men laughed loudly and continued up the street. There was no doubt that they were pirates!

## Chapter Three

Barbie, Midge, and Teresa continued their walk without saying a word.

The three women reached Teresa's home just as the sun began to set. From Teresa's front porch, the *Seaflower* could be seen, tall and proud in the bay. Dr. Dawson had come ashore to make plans for his new hospital, but the captain and many of the crew were still on board.

"Well, I was beginning to worry about you," Dr. Dawson said. He greeted his daughter with a kiss. "There are all kinds of **scoundrels** about, even in this island paradise."

Midge nodded. "I know what you mean," she said. She took a deep breath. Then she told him everything that had happened that afternoon.

Dr. Dawson listened to every word. His face was grim. "I must tell the captain at once," he told them. Then he turned to Teresa. "The navy ship will no doubt be put under orders to capture Red Beak. It won't be safe for Midge and Barbie to be on board. Is it all right if they stay here with you?"

"Of course," Teresa answered quickly. "I was just about to invite all of you to stay."

"Have you a boat I can take to reach the *Seaflower?*" Dr. Dawson asked. "It's still anchored offshore. The sooner the navy knows this information, the better our chances of catching that scoundrel."

"We have two boats," Teresa replied. "But my brothers have taken them fishing. They may not be back until very late."

Dr. Dawson had no choice but to wait.

In bed that night, Midge couldn't sleep. She was thinking about Teresa and her family. If only the navy could find the pirates' hideout! She got up from her bed and looked out the window. The *Seaflower* was visible in the moonlight.

Midge rested her elbows on the windowsill and looked at the stars. The clear night sky was dotted with hundreds of tiny islands of white light. She thought about the map Mick was working on back on board. She decided to test her memory.

"Hmmm," she said to herself, scanning the night sky for familiar patterns of stars. "There's Ursa Major and the Big Dipper." Then Midge found a smaller grouping of stars in the sky. "And there's Ursa

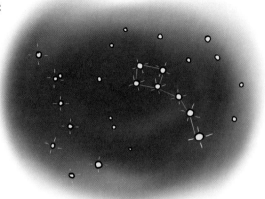

Minor, the Little Bear."

She smiled, happy that she had remembered them. Then her eyes widened. "Little Bear! Of course!"

Midge bounded across the room and lit a candle. With shaking hands, she quickly unrolled the map of the islands she had bought that morning. She studied the map. She was looking for a grouping of islands arranged in the same pattern as the stars in the sky. She laid her finger on a spot on the map. "Aha!" she cried out.

Midge grabbed her candle and ran to wake Barbie and Teresa. Stumbling out of bed, the two sleepy women pulled on their shawls. Then they

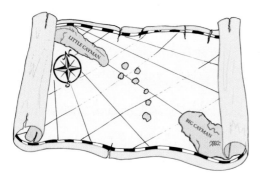

followed Midge back to her room. "What's wrong?" Barbie mumbled. "Look! Look!"

Midge cried, pointing to a tiny group of islands on her map. "Little Bear!"

"I don't understand," Teresa said, confused.

Midge explained, "These islands form a pattern similar to the stars in the constellation Ursa Minor."

"So?" Teresa asked.

"Midge, that's it!" Barbie exclaimed. "*Ursa Minor* means 'little bear'! So if the pirates are meeting at the mouth of the Little Bear, then one of these islands must be their hideout!" she continued.

Clutching the map, Midge cried, "We have to tell my father!"

The three friends rushed to find Dr. Dawson, but he was not in his room. Teresa woke Marta, the maid.

"The doctor is gone. Your brothers returned just a short while ago. The *Defiant* has been spotted. Your brothers and the doctor are going

to meet up with the navy," she told them. "They will join the *Seaflower* in chasing those awful pirates."

"Maybe we can catch them," Teresa suggested. "Let's go." She and Barbie and Midge raced out to the beach.

"Ladies! Come back! You are in your nightgowns!" the shocked maid called.

But the friends never looked back. Teresa led the way down the moonlit path to the beach. They ran barefoot across the warm sand down to the water's edge.

Off in the distance, they could see the *Seaflower* moving through the water.

"We're too late!" Teresa cried.

Chapter Four

With sinking hearts, Barbie, Midge, and
Teresa watched the *Seaflower* disappear over the
horizon.

"But they don't know where the hideout
is!" Barbie said in **frustration.** "Surely the
*Defiant* will lead them away from it!"

"If only we could sail," Midge sighed. She
looked at the map still clutched in her hand.
"Then we could catch up to the *Seaflower.*"

Barbie smiled. "Or we could even find the
hideout ourselves."

"We *do* have a boat," Teresa said. "My

brothers left the other sloop behind. That's it, right there." She pointed to a small, graceful ship with one large sail. It was anchored nearby.

"I know how to sail," Barbie offered.

"Me, too," Teresa added. "I used to sail all the time with my brothers."

"We could take the boat and use Midge's map to find the pirates' hideout," Barbie suggested. "The pirates will be sure to lead the navy away from the hideout. We should be safe, for a while, anyway."

Midge looked shocked. "We can't do that!"

Barbie replied, "But what about Teresa's family? We have a chance to help them. Besides, this could be our first *real* adventure."

Midge's eyes shone. "Let's do it!" she declared. "I can read the map while you two sail the boat."

"Count me in!" Teresa said breathlessly.

The sloop bobbed up and down in the water

not far from the shore. The friends shed their nightgowns on the beach and dove into the water in their underclothes. Soon they reached the small fishing boat and climbed aboard.

Teresa dug around in a trunk. She pulled out shirts and pants belonging to her brothers. "They smell a little fishy," she admitted, pulling a shirt over her head. "But at least they're dry."

Once they were dressed, the three set to work, sailing toward the pirates' hideout. "I've always wanted a chance to sail myself," Barbie said, steering the boat. "But I never dreamed I'd do it dressed as

Mast

Sail

Boom

Tiller

Bow

Rudder

a fisherman in the middle of the night. And in

pirate waters!" she said with a chuckle.

Midge and Teresa agreed.

"What would my father say if he could see me now?" Midge wondered out loud.

Teresa laughed. "Be glad he can't."

The wind picked up, and the small boat began to move faster through the water. Midge lit an oil lamp and studied her map. She peered carefully at the night sky. "We should move west," she said at last, setting their course by the stars. Barbie grabbed the tiller and leaned hard. Slowly the boat turned.

"We're doing it!" Teresa said excitedly. "How long do you think it will take us to reach Little Bear?"

Barbie shook her head. "That depends on the wind," she answered.

They sailed until dawn, guided by the stars and a good, strong breeze. When the first rays of sunlight colored the sky pink, Barbie jumped up and shouted, "Land ho!" She grinned. "I've always wanted to say that."

A small island lay ahead of them. They turned the boat toward the beach.

"There are so many rocks," Teresa said in a worried voice. "We need to be careful not to hit any of them."

Midge checked the map. "There are four small islands here," she explained. "The hideout could be on any one of them. How will we know where to go?"

"Well," Barbie began, "tell us again what the mapmaker said, Midge."

Midge replied, "He said, 'The trade is made. Go to the mouth of the Little Bear.' "

"Hmmm," Barbie pondered. "Where could the 'mouth' be?"

"I think I know!" Teresa cried, peering through a spyglass. She pointed to a group of rocks on the island. "Do you see what I see?"

There was a large cave with two huge **boulders** on each side. Midge looked through the spyglass. "Those rocks look like a bear's head," she cried. "And that cave must be its mouth. We've found Red Beak's hideout. We have to sail into that cave!"

"Wait!" Barbie stopped her. "It's almost high tide. See how the water is rushing into that opening? Pretty soon the 'mouth' will be underwater. We'd be trapped. We will have to wait until low tide, when the water is shallow again."

"But that's six hours from now!" Teresa cried.

Everyone was disappointed. But they knew that Barbie was right.

"There might be another way into the cave," Barbie suggested. "Maybe we should drop anchor and swim ashore."

"We shouldn't leave the boat," Teresa said.

"If Red Beak and his crew show up, we'll need to get away, *fast!*"

They had no choice but to wait for the tide to go out again. It was frustrating to be so close to the hideout and not be able to go in. Midge spent the time studying the map. The sea around them was calm, and through the clear water, they could see a colorful coral reef.

"There have been a lot of shipwrecks around here," Teresa told Barbie and Midge. "These waters are full of sunken treasure: gold, jewelry, silver. Now only the fish can enjoy them."

Midge put down the map and picked up the spyglass. Suddenly she cried out, "The pirates are coming!" She gasped. "I can see the skull and crossbones of the Jolly Roger flag!"

34

## Chapter Five

Midge passed the spyglass to Barbie and Teresa. A large ship with tall sails was heading right toward the island. On the bow of the ship was the name *Defiant.*

The women sprang into action. Teresa pulled the anchor out of the water while Barbie and Midge tugged at the sail. Soon the little fishing boat was back in the open sea.

"Hang on! I'm going to turn us toward them," Barbie declared.

"What?" Midge and Teresa shouted at the same time.

"Barbie!" Teresa cried. "They'll see us! We have to get out of here!"

"Trust me," Barbie promised. "I know what I'm doing."

Barbie swung the tiller once more, and the boat cut through the water quickly. They no longer needed a spyglass to see the *Defiant*. It was right in front of them.

"We'll lead them away from the hideout," Barbie explained. "With any luck, the navy's ships will be following right behind them. If we can just distract Red Beak long enough, the navy may be able to catch them."

"I sure hope you're right," Teresa gulped.

By then the *Defiant* had caught sight of the small fishing boat. It began following the sloop at great speed. Several pirates were running on the deck of their ship, calling to one another and pointing.

"I don't see the *Seaflower* yet," Teresa told

Barbie. "And the pirates are getting closer!"

Midge bit her lip, thinking hard. Then she jumped up and pointed at another island in the distance. "Head that way, Barbie! My map shows a rock formation near the shoreline of that island," she said. "It will be underwater now, because the tide is high. If we can just lead Red Beak there . . ."

"The *Defiant* will hit the rocks and be stranded," Barbie finished. "But what about us? Won't we be in danger of the same thing happening to us?"

"Not if my map is right," Midge said, her voice filled with **determination.** "Our boat should be small and light enough to sail through a gap in the rocks."

There was no more time for talk, for the wind had picked up. The tall ship was almost on top of the tiny fishing boat. A red-faced pirate was leaning over the railing. He wore a black,

three-cornered hat and had a big, sunburned nose. It was Red Beak himself!

"Women?" Red Beak shouted in surprise. "Why, I'll teach you to come looking for my treasure! You'll pay for this! All of you!"

The fishing boat sped ahead of the pirate ship. The island was not far away now.

"Faster! Faster!" Teresa shouted, as Barbie held the tiller steady.

"The rocks are coming up," Midge warned. "We have to slow down."

"But Red Beak is right behind us!" Teresa cried. "We can't slow down now."

"We must!" Midge insisted. "I remember the positioning of the rocks from the map. We have to sail through the gap carefully."

Teresa lowered the sail and slowed the boat. She glanced over the bow. Sure enough, huge rocks lay just beneath the water's surface.

"Aha!" Red Beak shouted. "I have you now.

And a fine reward I'll get for your safe return!"

Barbie, Midge, and Teresa ignored him. They were trying to steer safely through the dangerous waters.

"Easy," Teresa advised. "There's a big rock coming up."

"We should be in the clear after that," Midge added, trying to sound hopeful.

They all held their breath as they passed over the huge, jagged rock. They heard a slight scraping sound on the bottom of the boat. Luckily, they didn't get stuck. Their boat was safe!

As soon as they had sailed away from the rock, they heard a shout from the *Defiant.*

"Turn back! Turn back!" Red Beak screamed to his crew. But it was too late. The *Defiant* slammed into the rock—hard! Big waves rolled out from under the ship, rocking the little fishing boat like a toy.

"You fools!" Red Beak shouted at his men.

"Look what you've done to my ship!" But all the shouting in the world wouldn't change things. The *Defiant* was stranded on the rocks and would sail no more. The pirates had no choice but to climb overboard and swim for the shore.

Barbie, Teresa, and Midge didn't wait to see what would happen next. They turned their boat back out to sea. The tide was on its way out now. It was time to go back to Little Bear.

## Chapter Six

The cave with the familiar cub ears on each side soon appeared in view. It was low tide, and the three women dropped anchor close to the cave. They lowered a small rowboat over the side and climbed in. In no time, they were inside the dark, rocky cave.

"Spooky," Teresa said. Her voice echoed in the darkness. Barbie was glad that they had remembered to bring their lantern with them.

When the water got too shallow to row anymore, the friends jumped out and waded to a sandy ledge. They were very glad to be wearing comfortable pants instead of long, heavy skirts.

They walked deeper into the cave. Suddenly Teresa cried out in pain. "Owww! My toe!" As she bent down to rub her foot, she called out again. "Barbie! Midge! Come here, quick!"

Teresa had stubbed her toe on a long crate half-buried in the sand. Painted in large letters on the top were the words *Dawson, M.D., Charleston, South Carolina.*

"Do you know what this is?" Teresa exclaimed. "These are the medicines that were stolen from the navy ship last month."

Digging in the sand with their hands, the friends were able to uncover the rest of the crate. They opened the heavy lid. Rows of medicine bottles gleamed in the dim light from the lantern. Not one was even cracked.

The medicines were not the only thing in Red Beak's cave. There were chests filled with golden coins, silver goblets, diamonds, and rubies! It was clear that Red Beak had been a very successful pirate for a very long time.

"Look," Barbie said, lifting a piece of paper from a chest filled with gold. "It's a bill of sale. Tell me again, Teresa, what does your family grow?"

"Sugarcane. And some rice. Why?" Teresa answered.

"This receipt is for the sale of sugar, purchased from the Rivera Plantation. It says here that it was traded on November 10, 1709," Barbie read aloud.

"Why, that's ours. And that date is just a few days before Red Beak captured our ship!" Teresa stated. "That must mean . . ."

"That all this gold belongs to your family," Barbie finished. "Teresa, you have

45

your fortune back!"

Teresa jumped up and hugged her friends joyfully. "It's a dream come true!" she cried.

Together, the three women loaded the medicines and as much of the family's gold as their little rowboat could hold. They hated to leave anything behind. But the tide was beginning to come in again.

The sail back to Teresa's home was smooth. As the boat neared the shore, they could see the *Seaflower* anchored in the bay. On the beach, people were racing to the water's edge.

"Midge! Barbie! Teresa! Thank goodness you're all right!" Dr. Dawson cried. He rushed through the water to meet them. "We were worried that you had been kidnapped by Red Beak!"

"We're fine," Midge assured him. The three women climbed out of the boat and waded through the waves together.

Then Midge declared, "And you needn't

worry about Red Beak anymore!"

Quickly the three women told the doctor about their adventure. They described their night of sailing and how they had tricked the *Defiant.* The doctor shook his head in amazement.

Just then the captain of the *Seaflower* came rushing down the beach to meet them.

"We lost sight of the *Defiant,*" the captain told the group. He hadn't yet heard the women's story. "Our ship was too heavy to keep up with it. I am sending my men out in smaller sloops to check the nearby islands. The important thing, though, is that these young ladies are safe."

Barbie grinned. "You can save yourself some trouble," she informed the captain. "The *Defiant* is stranded on a rock."

Teresa added, "Her crew had to swim ashore."

Unrolling her map, Midge pointed out the Little Bear. "You will find them on this island, right here." Then the three women repeated their tale to the captain.

When they were finished, the captain proudly shook their hands. "You have done a great service today," he told the brave women. "The navy has been trying to bring Red Beak to justice for a long time. There is a large reward for that buccaneer's capture. And as soon as he's behind bars, the reward is yours."

Midge and Barbie didn't even have to discuss it. "I know just what we should do with the reward money," Midge announced.

"We want Teresa and Dr. Dawson to have it to open their hospital here," Barbie added.

"Now we can buy more medicines and supplies!" Dr. Dawson exclaimed.

"Wait. The best is yet to come," Teresa added with a twinkle in her eye. "Close your eyes."

Dr. Dawson did as she said. Teresa reached into one of the crates and pulled out a bottle of **serum.** When the doctor felt the smooth, round bottle she placed in his hand, his eyes flew open.

"Our medicine! You found it!" he cried.

Midge read the label on the bottle. "For headache. Hmmm. Do you think I could have a dose of that? My head is throbbing! It's been a very long night and day."

"Of course, my dear," Dr. Dawson said, putting his arm around his tired daughter. "You all must get some rest."

Back at Teresa's house, Midge stretched out on the bed and closed her eyes. Her head was feeling a little better now that she was out of the sun.

"Poor Midge," she heard Barbie say.

"You'll be my first patient," Teresa said. "Let me get you a cloth for your head."

When Midge felt the cool, wet cloth on her forehead, she opened her eyes once more. She looked around and became confused. "Where am I?" she whispered.

Chapter Seven

"Oh, thank goodness!" Barbie cried. "You had us so worried, Midge!"

Midge sat up and blinked. Barbie and Teresa were kneeling beside her with concerned faces. Midge looked down. Instead of dirty fisherman's clothing, she was wearing shorts and sneakers. Instead of being in a soft bed on a tropical island, she was on the deck of a modern sailboat.

Midge rubbed her head. "Ow," she moaned. "What happened?"

"Don't you remember?" Teresa asked.

"Not really," Midge replied, frowning.

Barbie sat down on the deck. She pulled her baseball cap down to shade her eyes from the sun. "We decided to sail over to that island," she explained, looking off into the distance, "because you wanted to go exploring."

"But then the wind shifted," Teresa chimed in. "Barbie and I swung the sail's boom around fast to catch the breeze. Barbie told you to duck, Midge, but it was too late."

"The wooden boom hit you in the head," Barbie finished.

Now Midge remembered. It was the **twentieth century.** And she was on vacation with her friends. The three women were sailing their own boat around the Cayman Islands.

Midge rubbed her sore head and stood up slowly. She thought about everything: the *Defiant*, Red Beak, the treasure. "Had it all been just a dream?" she thought. "It seemed so real!"

Teresa told Barbie, "We had better sail back

to Grand Cayman. I think Midge should see a doctor."

Barbie agreed. "I hear the island has a terrific hospital."

"Hospital?" Midge asked. "How long have I been out?"

"Only a minute or two," Barbie answered. "But we were so worried, it seemed like you were out for centuries."

Midge laughed. "You have no idea!"